MIDDLE SCHOOL
HOLLYWOOD 101

JAMES PATTERSON is the internationally bestselling author of the highly praised Middle School books, *Homeroom Diaries*, *Kenny Wright: Superhero*, *Jacky Ha-Ha*, and the I Funny, Treasure Hunters, House of Robots, Maximum Ride, Confessions, Witch & Wizard and Daniel X series. James Patterson has been the most borrowed author in UK libraries for the past nine years in a row and his books have sold more than 325 million copies worldwide, making him one of the biggest-selling authors of all time. He lives in Florida.

THE
MIDDLE
SCHOOL
SERIES

THE WORST YEARS OF MY LIFE
(with Chris Tebbetts)

This is the insane story of my first year at middle school, when I, Rafe Khatchadorian, took on a real-life bear (sort of), sold my soul to the school bully, and fell for the most popular girl in school. Come join me, if you dare...

GET ME OUT OF HERE!
(with Chris Tebbetts)

We've moved to the big city, where I'm going to a super-fancy art school. The first project is to create something based on our exciting lives. But I have a BIG problem: my life is TOTALLY BORING. It's time for Operation Get a Life.

MY BROTHER IS A BIG, FAT LIAR
(with Lisa Papademetriou)

So you've heard all about my big brother, Rafe, and now it's time to set the record straight. I'm NOTHING like my brother. (Almost) EVERYTHING he says is a Big Fat Lie. And my book is 100 times better than Rafe's. I'm Georgia, and it's time for some payback... Khatchadorian style.

HOW I SURVIVED BULLIES, BROCCOLI, AND SNAKE HILL
(with Chris Tebbetts)

I'm excited for a fun summer at camp—until I find out it's a summer *school* camp. There's no fun and games here, I have a bunk mate called Booger Eater (it's pretty self-explanatory), and we're up against the kids from the "Cool Cabin"... there's gonna be a whole lotta trouble!

ULTIMATE SHOWDOWN
(with Julia Bergen)

Who would have thought that we—Rafe and Georgia—would ever agree on anything? That's right—we're writing a book together. Discover: Who has the best advice on BULLIES? Who's got all the right DANCE MOVES? Who's the cleverest Khatchadorian in town? And the best part? We want you to be part of the fun too!

SAVE RAFE!
(with Chris Tebbetts)

I'm in worse trouble than ever! I need to survive a gut-bustingly impossible outdoor excursion so I can return to school next year. Watch me as I become "buddies" with the scariest girl on the planet, raft down the rapids on a deadly river, and ultimately learn the most important lesson of my life.

JUST MY ROTTEN LUCK
(with Chris Tebbetts)

I'm heading back to the place it all began: Hills Village Middle School, but only if I take "special" classes... If that wasn't bad enough, when I somehow land a place on the school football team, I find myself playing alongside none other than the biggest bully in school, Miller the Killer!

MIDDLE SCHOOL
SCHOOL
HOLLYWOOD
101

JAMES PATTERSON
AND MARTIN CHATTERTON

1 3 5 7 9 10 8 6 4 2

Young Arrow
20 Vauxhall Bridge Road
London SW1V 2SA

Young Arrow is part of the Penguin Random House group of companies
whose addresses can be found at global.penguinrandomhouse.com

First published by Young Arrow in 2016

www.penguin.co.uk

A CIP catalogue record for this book is
available from the British Library

ISBN 9781784756819

Typeset by Roger Walker
Printed and bound in Great Britain by Clays Ltd, St Ives Plc

Penguin Random House is committed to a sustainable future for our
business, our readers and our planet. This book is made from Forest
Stewardship Council® certified paper.

MIDDLE SCHOOL

SCHOOL

HOLLYWOOD
101

CHAPTER 1

THE REVENGE OF KHATCHADORZILLA

"**I** said, *seaweed and sable*, you idiot! Not *wheatgrass and chai*!" Hollywood teen heart-throb movie star Trey Kernigan, his perfect blond hair vibrating in fury, his perfect white teeth glinting in the Malibu sun, snarled at his personal assistant's assistant, Zuki. He hurled the smoothie across the deck of his multimillion-dollar beachside pad. "Get me what I *asked* for, *understand*? Or you'll be looking for another job, *Zucchini*, or whatever your dumb name is!"

The sobbing Zuki swept up the remains of the smoothie and scuttled off to the kitchen in search of seaweed and sable. Trey Kernigan adjusted his expensive shades, sat back down on the deck, and crossed his legs.

Zuki had completely *ruined* his Monday-morning yoga. He decided he'd sack her. Or get his personal assistant to do it. Or sack them both. Either way, that smoothie-ruining loser would be flipping burgers out with all the ordinary people before sundown.

Trey took a long, deep breath, plugged in his Peruvian monk chant music, and tried to refocus his chakra. Life was just *sooo* hard. Honestly, some days it just wasn't worth a Hollywood teen heart-throb movie star getting up in the morning.

"Umdoolalaley*aaaah*," chanted Trey. "Umdoolalaley*aaah*."

A mile out from the beach something stirred below the waves.

Something big and green and scaly with lots and lots of teeth. You know the kind of thing: like a giant lizard-dragon monster deal.

The only difference between regular giant lizard-dragon monsters and *this* one was that this one looked almost exactly like a kid called Rafe Khatchadorian. Here's a pic of both side by side.

Rafe Khatchadorian

Lizard-dragon monster

See what I mean? I mean, I know that's kind of random, but trust me, it's important. Go with it.

3

Anyway, this giant lizard-dragon monster that looked almost exactly like a kid called Rafe Khatchadorian came up out of the water and headed straight for Trey Kernigan's beachside pad.

"ROOOOOAAAAAARRRRRRR!!" roared the giant lizard-dragon monster stomping all over the beach umbrellas, the drink coolers...and Nate and Carol Urmgartssen who were visiting from Salt Lake City and who made the big mistake of thinking the giant lizard-dragon monster was some kind of Hollywood tourist attraction.

Everyone else screamed and ran.

Except Trey Kernigan. He had his eyes closed and his ears filled with the sound of Peruvian monk chants. It wasn't until a shadow fell across him that Trey opened his eyes.

And immediately wished he hadn't.

The giant lizard-dragon monster reached down with a slimy claw and lifted Trey Kernigan up by the scruff of his Armani dressing gown.

"Why?" wailed Trey. "I'm just a harmless Hollywood teen superstar with perfect teeth and hair! I never hurt anyone! Why? *WHY?*"

"Jeanne Galletta," said the giant lizard-dragon monster.

"Who?" said Trey as the giant lizard-dragon monster dropped the Hollywood teen heart-throb movie star into its mouth.

"Doesn't matter," said the giant lizard-dragon monster as it scarfed Trey Kernigan down like a cheeseball and headed back to the ocean.

UN, DOS, TREY

Yeah, okay, I know. You're way ahead of me. Trey Kernigan didn't get eaten by any giant lizard-dragon. That was all in my head, just like you'd all figured out.

I mean, Trey Kernigan's real enough but all the rest was so much hooey. I'm guessing that if you're reading this you probably know me well enough by now to know that I sometimes let my imagination run away with me. Or as Leo the Silent, my not-quite-imaginary brother,* puts it: I'm nuts. And if you don't know me, I'm Rafe Khatchadorian: middle schooler, artist, occasional dish pig at Swifty's Diner.

* For anyone who doesn't know, Leo *was* my brother but he died when I was small. Sometimes he pops up and gives me advice, whether I need it or not.

Anyway, for all I know, Trey Kernigan's sucking down a seaweed and sable smoothie right now. Does anyone know what sable actually *is*, by the way? I've never met Trey Kernigan. I mean, I live in Hills Village, Nowheresville. How am *I* ever gonna meet a movie star? Hills Village hasn't even got a movie theater.

"So what was all that about Kernigan?"

See? That's what Leo does. He gets me back on track. Leo looks after me.

The problem with Trey Kernigan is this: I flat out don't like the dude.

I know that might seem kind of weird seeing as how I don't know him, but if you went to school one day and The Best Girl In The World (aka Jeanne Galletta) had Trey Kernigan's photo taped to all her books and bags and stuff, what would *you* think?

Exactly.

To make things worse, Jeanne's bestie, Molly Dufresne, told me Jeanne's bedroom is totally covered with Trey posters, and Trey Kernigan is all Jeanne talks about. *All the time.*

How does an average Joe like me compete with that?

Well, I'll tell you how: I can't.

Not unless I happen to be a giant mutant reptile who knows exactly where Trey Kernigan's Malibu beach house is. Which I'm not and I don't, so it's back to dull old reality for R. Khatchadorian and the start of another ordinary, completely average, MASSIVELY sucky Hills Village Middle School week.

CHAPTER 3

NEW KID ON THE BLOCK

Okay, if there's one thing that could make a Monday morning at Hills Village Middle School better—besides a Snow Day, or an outbreak of bubonic plague, or something closing the whole place down—it's the arrival of a new kid.

New kids arriving at school always make things more interesting. For everyone else, that is. For the new kid, being "the new kid" is pretty close to being lunch at the lion enclosure. Fresh meat. I could almost feel the lions circling. Or Miller the Killer, anyway...which is pretty much the same thing. At least the new kid was a girl. Miller was a bit easier on girls.

"This is Kristen Doe, everyone," said Ms. Donatello, smiling brightly and pointing to a girl wearing black-framed glasses and looking like she'd rather be at the dentist. "I'm sure you're all going to give Kristen a very warm Hills Village Middle School welcome."

There were a few grunts and a couple of laughs. Someone lobbed a ball of paper from the back of the class and it bounced off Kristen's head. Everyone laughed and she turned bright red and started scribbling furiously in a little black notebook. I wondered what *that* was all about. While Ms. Donatello went to the back of the class to start her investigation into The Great Paper-Throwing Incident of 2016, I got up and walked over to the new kid.

"Don't mind those idiots," I whispered. "We're not all like that."

I wasn't expecting much. Which was just as well, because I didn't get much. But Kristen nodded.

"Thanks," she said in a voice about two decibels higher than a mouse's burp. Up close she had amazing blue eyes hidden behind her glasses. I looked into them and felt—and look, I know how lame-o this is gonna sound—dizzy, like I'd stared into the sun too long. Kristen had eyes like an Icelandic glacier. Okay, the nearest I'd been to Iceland was watching a documentary on minke whale conservation (it was a dull TV night), but that's what Kristen's eyes reminded me of. Not minke whales—Icelandic glaciers.

I knew right then that I would do everything in my power to be The Coolest Kid in Hills

Village Middle School and impress Kristen more than she'd ever been impressed before.

"No problem," I said. "Any time."

It was a good start. A really good start. For once in my uncool life I'd stayed cool around a girl. I strolled back to my desk, and did that sort of pointy thing with your finger like a salute. Kristen smiled and I sat down.

And farted.

CHAPTER 4

THE FART TO END ALL FARTS

It was a loud fart.

Like MEGA LOUD. Like a jet engine had just started up loud. Like King Kong loud. Rock band loud. I could almost see the walls of the classroom vibrating.

And long.

So long. Way, way, *way* long. I mean, no one was timing it or anything, but I reckon this fart must have lasted about three days.

Later on, of course, I figured out that it had been a fart of probably just above average length (and no, I don't know the average length of time a fart lasts). But at the time it went on. And on. And on.

And on.

It was The Fart To End All Farts.

When the last note finally died away there was a short, shocked silence. And then the whole class went nuts—and I mean, they totally, 100 percent *lost it*. They laughed, they screamed, they whooped, they hollered. I saw one kid laugh so much that snot came out his nose. Even Ms. Donatello looked like she was going to explode.

Kristen looked at me and I felt every last shred of cool shrivel up and disappear like snowflakes on a red-hot griddle. Which, coincidentally, was the exact temperature of my face.

Of course, it wasn't me.

I might be many things but a public farter isn't one of them. What happened was that Miller the Killer had put a fart cushion on my chair... and then somehow managed to whip it back off while everyone was busy peeing themselves laughing.

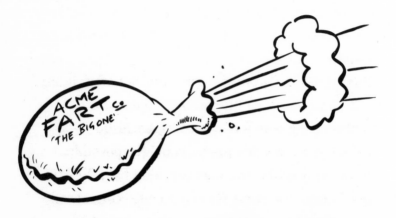

There was nothing I could do except sit there and watch my dignity drain away.

Goodbye, dignity. So long, Kristen.

CHAPTER 5

WHO iS SPARTACUS?

Trying to impress a girl you like after being outed as a public farter—even when the whole thing was a total set-up by Miller—is difficult. In fact it's pretty much impossible. Especially when the fart was The Fart To End All Farts. It was all HVMS was talking about. Someone even made a Facebook page: "Rafe's Giant Fart." I wouldn't have been surprised to see it being turned into a movie.

I decided to forget all about Kristen Doe.

I'd become a hermit, go find a cave in Tibet, and think deep, wise thoughts about Life and all that kind of stuff. I'd grow a long beard and never see Kristen Doe ever again.

But those glacier-blue eyes kept popping up. I mean, in my head—Kristen's *actual* eyes didn't. That would have been *weird*.

No, what I mean is that those eyes did something unusual to me. They forced me to overcome the single greatest obstacle in a middle school kid's life: embarrassment.

You know what it's like, right? Embarrassment mostly stops kids doing *anything*. But so powerful were Kristen's eyes that only three days after the fart incident I got up enough courage to try again.

It was at lunch. Kristen was sitting at a table not far from Losers Corner.

Losers Corner? Every school has a Losers Corner, don't they? It's where the kids who aren't real popular with the popular kids sit for lunch. I mean, who decides who gets to be popular? Do the popular kids get issued with special tickets or something when they arrive that first day at school?

"Good morning, Susie Kendricks! Here's your Popular Kid voucher. It entitles you to a mostly hassle-free school life and an easy ride. Lunch? Sure, sit anywhere you like, as long as you don't go anywhere near Losers Corner, or talk to Rafe Khatchadorian."

You probably already figured that Losers Corner is where I sit. Anyway, this particular day I had decided I was going to speak to Kristen no matter what. I just had to wait for the right time.

I waited.

And waited.

And waited. It wasn't me, you understand? That right time just didn't happen.

And then I got my chance.

Vice Principal Stonecase was making her security rounds when she spotted a rip in Kristen Doe's jeans. Now, nothing floats Stonecase's boat more than some eeny-weeny, teeny-tiny school clothing violation.

"Doe!" roared Stonecase, rearing up onto her hind legs and breathing fire through her ears. "Those jeans are in clear violation of Hills Village Middle School clothing code forty-three, subsection three, paragraph two!"

Kristen remained seated, shocked, helpless. And adorable.

"I...I..." she stuttered.

There was a long silence and then, as Stonecase

Rex was about to hit Kristen with everything she had, I stood up and shouted:

"I am Spartacus!" Everyone looked at me.

"You're not Spartacus," said Stonecase. "You're Rafe Khatchadorian."

"It's from a movie," I said. "*Spartacus*. He's a slave and..."

She looked at me blankly. So did everyone else. In the movie I was talking about, once someone stands up and says "I am Spartacus," everyone else does the same. Kind of like everyone sticking up for each other.

Except now, no one was doing *anything*. There were no other Spartacuses. Spartaci?

"Oh, forget it," I said. I reached down and grabbed the pocket of my own jeans, which had a little tear in one corner, and gave it an almighty pull.

What was *supposed* to happen was that my pocket would rip off and I would be standing shoulder to shoulder with Kristen, two clothing-code violators side by side. She could look at me with those blue eyes and we'd be BFF.

But I'd clearly misjudged the strength of my jeans.

The pocket did come off. That bit worked just fine.

But so did everything else north of my knees. I stood there in my boxer shorts—the ones with pictures of Buzz and Woody from *Toy Story* on them that Grandma Dotty gave me last Christmas. The only clean ones in my drawer that morning.

I caught a glimpse of Jeanne Galletta staring at me from behind her bag—the one with the photo of Trey Kernigan on the front. Kernigan's perfect face seemed to be smiling at me.

I'd been embarrassed by The Fart To End All Farts, but this took things to a whole new level.

CHAPTER 6

RAFE KHATCHADORIAN, HIPSTER

"That was real kind of you," said a voice. "Thanks, Spartacus."

I looked up. It was Kristen.

I was sitting way off in the corner of the football field, out of sight of anyone and anything connected to Hills Village Middle School. If I could've I'd have relocated to Mars. I was wearing a pair of what can only be described as "slacks" that Stonecase had dug up from some Lost Property coffin she kept somewhere in the back of her dungeon. They'd been fashionable once. Say, around 1990.

"Nice threads," said Kristen, nodding at my slacks. "Hipster."

I was about to say something sarcastic when I realized Kristen meant it. She really thought the pants were cool. I looked at them again. Nope. They were still things even Mr. Fanucci would have turned his nose up at. Maybe that was Kristen's point.

"This girl's standing there and you're thinking about pants?" said Leo. He shook his head sadly and then faded out of view.

"You the only sane kid in this place?" said Kristen.

"Er, yeah," I said. "There was this one other kid, but he left. Since then it's just been me." I had to admit, that wasn't a bad comeback for me. Considering.

Kristen laughed. The sound was like the tinkle of a sun-dappled woodland stream across smooth rocks. Or something poetic, anyway.

"You wanna hang out?" said Kristen. "Go see a movie?"

"HAHAHAHAHAHAHA!" I laughed, but Kristen wasn't joking. I gave myself a mental slap across my mental face. Get real, Khatchadorian! This was an actual girl with actual Icelandic-glacier eyes actually asking me to the movies.

"Sure," I said. "Only, we don't have no movie theater round these parts."

I had no idea why I was speaking like some hick from a bad TV show. *Round these parts*? Where did *that* come from?

Kristen looked shocked, and not just by my accent. She lifted her dark bangs out of her eyes and looked at me. "You're kidding, right? Tell me you're kidding. No movie theater? None?"

I shook my head. "Nope. Not kidding."

"Man," muttered Kristen. "What do you guys *do* out here?"

I made a decision. I felt like I was one of those guys in the movies who has to defuse a bomb. Red wire or blue wire? One wrong move and I'd have blown my chance with Kristen.

"We could always watch something round at my shack. We gotten a TV that works, mostly. Color one and everything. I think Momma's even got one a them VCR kay-ssette tape ma-chines."

This time I was deliberately speaking like that. Just so you know.

"A TV *and* a VCR?" said Kristen. "Wow, you Hills Village guys really know how to live." She smiled. "Okay, Spartacus, we got a deal."

CHAPTER 7

ME AND ICELANDIC EYES

And just like that, me and Kristen started hanging out.

We watched movies round at my house and Mom only scored a seven on the EMQS (Embarrassing Mom Questions Scale). Even if Mom had hit a ten it would still have been worth it.

Because Kristen was *waaay* cool.

I felt like I'd known her all my life. Or at least for a while. I don't buy all that previous-life stuff, but with Kristen it sure felt like I'd known her before I *actually* knew her.

And, unbelievably, I was pretty sure *she* liked me. I know! Go figure.

We liked the same movies, mostly, and the same TV shows.

She really *knew* about all that stuff, too. She talked about them in an interesting way.

Then, just when I thought she couldn't get any more perfect, I discovered that Kristen also hated Trey Kernigan.

"Man, I *hate* that guy," she said one day when she caught sight of Kernigan's face on Jeanne's lunch box. "I hate his big dumb perfect teeth and his big dumb perfect hair. I hate his voice, his movies, everything. Yeuuch! What a total creep."

Even without her Icelandic eyes, hating Trey Kernigan would have made her Number One in my book. With Kristen it almost sounded personal. I mean, I couldn't stand the guy, but Kristen really sounded like she didn't like the dude.

Everything was great.

It couldn't last.

CHAPTER 8

DON'T BLOW IT

It didn't last.

The "everything being great," I mean. It never does.

For a week or so we went to school, hung out, watched movies, ate nachos. But I noticed that I actually wasn't getting to know much about Kristen. Not really.

We never went to her place. I hadn't met her mom or dad...I didn't even know if she *had* a mom or dad. I could have asked, but the right time for that never really came around. It would have felt too much like I was some kind of detective.

I didn't know where she was from. If things
came up in conversation, she'd sometimes say
she'd been to someplace or other. Weird places,
too, like Paris or Hawaii. I mean, not that those
places are weirder than anywhere else, just that
it was weird she seemed to know a lot of stuff
about them. Hawaii in particular.

I guess she could have been from Hawaii.
People *do* live there. It's just that Kristen didn't
look like she was from Hawaii. She just didn't
seem the Hawaii type.

"Like *you* know what the Hawaii type is," said Leo. "You ain't even sure where Hawaii *is*. Chill, bro. Relax. Kristen's cool. Don't blow it."

I'm not sure why Leo was talking like a rapper, but since he was in my imagination I guess that was my fault. Either way, he was right.

I needed to relax. Not. Blow. It.

"Kristen," I said one Saturday. We were sprawled all over the couch playing a computer game—one of the ones your parents don't like, but Mom was at work so that was okay. "How come you know so much about Hawaii?"

"I don't want to talk about it," said Kristen. She stared at the screen, concentrating.

A few minutes went by. We fought our way out of an alien incubation pod. The only sounds were of laser cannons and exploding aliens. I could feel another question bubbling just under the surface. I forced it back down.

"But where *are* you from?" I blurted out suddenly.

Kristen put down her controller and walked out without saying another word.

I'd blown it.

CHAPTER 9

THINGS GET WEIRD

I didn't see Kristen all week. I mean, I saw her at school, in class, scribbling away in that black notebook, eating lunch in Losers Corner, but I didn't *hang* with her, we didn't have fun like we used to.

By Friday I'd decided I was going to say something. Apologize for being a nosy jerk. Make everything cool. Be Spartacus again.

I'd planned to catch her at the school gate. She'd always made a big deal about walking home from school alone. This time I was going to be there.

But our class was late getting out. By the time I got to the gate Kristen was almost out of sight. She disappeared round the corner of Laurel Boulevard and I ran after her.

As I came round the corner, Kristen was standing waiting at the next corner. I was about to call her name when a gleaming black, brand-new, expensive-looking SUV with blacked-out windows slid to a halt next to Kristen. A guy wearing a smart black suit got out and held the back door open for her. She stepped inside and the SUV pulled away.

"Well, *that* was weird," said Leo.

Leo was dead right. It was weird. And it was about to get a whole lot weirder.

CHAPTER 10

THINGS GET WEIRDER

I didn't get much sleep that night. Thoughts of Kristen and black SUVs swirled around my head. When I got to my Saturday-morning shift at Swifty's, I was not operating at FRP (Full Rafe Potential).

ZRP (Zero Rafe Potential)

MRP (Mid Rafe Potential)

FRP (Full Rafe Potential)

About halfway through the morning, I looked up through the serving hatch and saw a shiny black SUV pull up outside.

Kristen!

This was my chance. I was gonna fix things. I was not going to do my usual Rafe thing and stand back like a dummy. I was going to *act*!

I took off my dishwashing apron (that would *not* have been a cool look), washed my hands, and slipped out into the diner. Swifty wasn't around so no one yelled at me for taking a break.

At first I didn't see Kristen, but then I caught a glimpse of her wedged into a corner booth with three other people. Lou, one of the Swifty's waitresses, was taking their breakfast order.

"Are they her family?" asked Leo. I shrugged.

To be honest they didn't look like they'd be *anyone's* family.

Sitting next to Kristen was a big guy who looked like a grizzly bear in a suit. A very expensive suit. This guy had muscles on his muscles. Across the table from Kristen was a nervy-looking guy with a black beard who was tapping a finger on a salt shaker. Next to him was a thin woman with long shiny hair. They were all wearing sunglasses. It was raining outside.

I waited for Lou to head back to the kitchen.

"Hey," I said as I approached the table.

Grizzly Bear Guy stood up and put a hand the size of Minneapolis on my chest. I looked up. His head was somewhere up by the ceiling. "Back off," he growled in a voice that sounded like he gargled with nails.

"Easy, Hector," said the dude with the beard. He looked up and flashed a smile that wasn't a smile at me. It was there and gone almost before I had time to register it.

"What d'you want, kid? We already placed the order."

"I, uh, I…er, well, I…" My words seemed to get all stuck in my throat. The thin woman snorted and I could feel myself turning red. I noticed Miller the Killer watching me. "I just wanted to talk to Kristen," I eventually managed to say.

"Who?" said the beardy guy. "Oh, right, Kristen." He smirked and looked out of the window.

Kristen still hadn't said anything. She hadn't even looked up.

"Hi, Kristen," I said.

Now Kristen did look up. She was about to say something when Beardy Guy cut in.

"Look, kid, Kristen doesn't want to talk to anyone right now, isn't that right, Kristen?"

Kristen put her head down and nodded.

"So you can just scoot on back to wherever you came from, okay?"

"Er…" I said.

"Now," said Grizzly Bear Guy.

"I'm leaving Hills Village," said Kristen quickly. "We won't be seeing each other again, Spartacus."

Beardy Guy laughed. "'Spartacus'? What kind of

a name is 'Spartacus'?" He shook his head. "Okay, *Spartacus*, you heard the little lady. Scram. Skedaddle. Vamoose."

"Kristen?" I said.

But she kept her head down and her Icelandic eyes hidden behind her sunglasses. I skulked off back to the kitchen.

And Miller the Killer had seen the whole thing.

News of my total, 100 percent humiliation would be round Hills Village Middle School before you could say "loser."

CHAPTER 11

INVASION OF THE QUINOA EATERS

I'm going to do one of my famous *FRRRRP*s now.

FRRRRRP!

No, that's not another Fart To End All Farts. (I thought I'd explained that was all Miller's doing?) This *FRRRRP* is a sound effect and it means I'm fast-forwarding. *FRRRRP!*...just like that, *FRRRRP!* past a couple of miserable months.

There. That's better. I skipped right past all those boring, non-movie-watching, non-nachos-eating, non-*Kristen* days and popped out back at Swifty's on another Saturday morning. I somehow survived the UTTER HUMILIATION of MtK telling everyone about Kristen blanking me, and came out the other side older, wiser, and sadder.

The reason I'm *FRRRRP*ing through to this particular Saturday is that this was the Saturday that Swifty's got taken over by aliens.

At least, that's what it seemed like.

They started showing up around eight, and by ten the entire place was stuffed to overflowing with them. They talked loudly, wore strange-looking clothes, had unpronounceable names, and asked for meals that could only have been eaten by people from Saturn or Jupiter: quinoa porridge, pressed wildflower chai risotto, lime-tinged seafoam, buffalo milk. Swifty's doesn't cater for aliens so they all had to make do with regular burgers, dogs, fries, and coffee.

Hills Valley had been invaded.

By Hollywood.

CHAPTER 12

HOORAY FOR HOLLYWOOD!

Yep, you heard me.

Hollywood. As in the movies, Oscars, actors.

"What's going on?" I asked Swifty. You could tell how weird a day it was because he didn't say anything about me being outside the kitchen.

"They're filming a movie here." Swifty shook his head in disbelief. "Right here in Hills Village! *Average Joe*, it's called. Some kind of superhero deal."

I was about to ask Swifty for more details when he darted off to try and figure out if his strawberry shortcake was gluten-free.

I looked out of the window. Outside the parking lot was full of all kinds of trailers and

lighting rig trucks and cars, most of them with
the famous Megalith Movie logo or *Average Joe*
written on the side in a kind of squiggly green
writing. Looked as though Swifty's information
was right.

Before I could digest the MIND-BOGGLING
news that Hills Village was now part of
Hollywood, I caught a glimpse of a shiny black
SUV with tinted windows and, even though I was
completely, totally, 100 percent OVER Kristen, I
couldn't help but wonder if *she'd* shown up too.

Then I saw two more SUVs just like the one I'd seen Kristen in and realized that those kind of swanky cars would be common in Hollywood.

The news about *Average Joe* spread outwards from Swifty's across Hills Village like wildfire. I'd never seen a wildfire, but I'm assuming they move pretty quickly. In any case, before you could yell "Action!" people started drifting up to take a look for themselves. Pretty soon, Swifty had to put Big Tony on the door to make sure only paying customers were allowed in.

"Rafe!"

I turned around and saw Swifty at the till, jerking a thumb in the direction of the kitchen. "Back on the suds, kid!" he yelled. "We're runnin' outta dishes!"

I nodded and turned round.

And bumped straight into someone who'd just come through the doors.

Indie Starr.

CHAPTER 13

YOU LOOK LIKE A GOLDFISH

Indie Starr!

Indie Starr, one of the biggest teen movie stars on the planet, was right there in Swifty's!

I went hot and then cold and then hot again. For a horrible moment I thought I might faint.

Indie Starr was wearing a huge pair of sunglasses and her face was framed by her trademark long blond hair. Everything she had on looked like it cost more than Swifty's Diner. There seemed to be a soft, golden glow around her, like someone was following her round with a spotlight.

There were a whole bunch of people in
sunglasses and suits there too, but all I saw was
a kind of blur. I guess if Indie Starr's around,
everyone else is hardly noticeable. While I stood,
goggling like an idiot, a woman in white pushed
past me. "Out of the way," she hissed. "Miss Starr
wants to sit down."

A big dude in a suit with a little phone thing wrapped around his ear pushed me to one side. "Don't crowd Miss Starr," he growled, and I stood back. I'd seen the big guy before in Swifty's. Hector? Was that his name? And if it *was* Hector and he was now with Indie Starr, what had he been doing with Kristen last time I'd seen him? I couldn't figure it out.

Right at that moment, Indie Starr passed me. She lifted a finger, put it under my chin, and closed my mouth.

"You look like a goldfish," she whispered. "Not cool."

She moved on and, like everyone else, I watched Indie Starr and her entourage head toward a booth. The whole place had gone quiet, even the movie people.

"Khatchadorian!" yelled Swifty.

The shout seemed to break the spell and conversation started up again as I headed back to the kitchen. I started de-glooping a stack of plates the height of Mount Rushmore but, even more than usual, my mind wasn't on the job.

Indie Starr!

I was so wrapped up in my Hollywood daydream that I didn't notice how much time had passed. Then a shadow fell across the sink.

I looked round and saw the big guy-who-might-have-been-Hector.

"I didn't mean to—" I began, but the big guy-who-might-have-been-Hector held up a paw.

"Miss Starr has requested a meeting outside in her car, sir," said Hector—I'm gonna call him plain old Hector because it's kind of boring calling him the big guy-who-might-have-been-Hector.

"With me?" I looked around, half expecting to see he'd been talking to someone else. Someone famous. Hector just nodded.

"This way, if you please. Miss Starr doesn't like to be kept waiting."

CHAPTER 14

MISS STARR WILL SEE YOU NOW

I walked out of Swifty's in a daze.

Hector held open the door for me and we walked quickly across to one of the shiny black cars. He went to the back door and opened it. I looked at him nervously and he gestured for me to get in. Was I going to be whacked for being rude to a movie star?

I put my head inside, feeling like one of those dudes at the circus putting their head in a lion's mouth.

There, sitting on the backseat, was Indie Starr herself.

"I am so sorry, Miss Starr," I said. "I didn't mean to—"

"Get in," she muttered impatiently. "And quit apologizing. You didn't do anything."

I got in. Indie Starr turned to Hector.

"We'll be five minutes, Hector," she said.

"Mr. DeMartelli said not to—"

Indie Starr cut right across Hector. "I don't *care* what Mr. DeMartelli said! Go!"

"Of course, Miss Starr," said Hector. He closed the car door and walked off about ten paces, where he stood waiting like some kind of robot.

"You have to be firm with them," said Indie Starr. "Otherwise they'll boss you around."

I nodded, like I gave orders to bodyguards every day.

"So, anyway," I said, "like I was saying, I—"

Indie Starr shifted in her seat and looked at me. "Still the same old Spartacus," she said.

"Yeah...I guess. Eh? *What?*"

Indie Starr took off her sunglasses, put on a

pair of regular black glasses, and smiled. I heard a funny buzzing sound in my ears.

"It's me," said Indie Starr. "Kristen."

Then everything went black.

CHAPTER 15

THE OLD CLARK KENT SWITCHEROO

Before Indie Starr pulled the old Clark Kent Switcheroo by putting on glasses and becoming instantly recognizable as my old friend Kristen Doe, I'd always sorta, y'know, *laughed* at those superhero movies where the superhero hides their identity by wearing or not wearing glasses.

A Superhero

Not A Superhero

Now I knew I was dead wrong.

I had had *no* idea that Indie Starr was Kristen, or Kristen Indie Starr, or *what* was going on. I only knew that it was one of the biggest shocks in my life.

Which was probably why I fainted.

Okay, that's not something I'm too proud of so I'd appreciate it if you didn't pass that around. That sort of information can be dynamite in the wrong hands. Like Miller the Killer's, for example.

Anyway, it was only for a couple of minutes. Three, tops.

When I opened my eyes, Indie...Kristen... whatever her name really was...was looking at me with a worried expression.

"You okay, Spartacus?"

I nodded and sat up straight. "I'm fine." I looked at her. "So what do I call you? 'Indie'? 'Miss Starr'? 'Kristen'?"

"Indie will do," she said. "Believe it or not, that's my real name. The Indie bit, not 'Starr.' That was Vic's idea."

I didn't say anything. Now I was coming round from the shock of discovering the long-lost love of my life was a movie star, I was getting pretty riled about being kept in the dark. *Now* I understood why she knew so much about the movies. And all the Hawaii stuff! Indie had been in that Hawaii cop show for two years!

"I can see you need an explanation," said Indie (it was going to take me a while to get used to calling her that).

So she told me.

CHAPTER 16

I'M GONNA PUT YOU IN THE MOVIES. KIND OF

"I got the *Average Joe* job about six months ago," said Indie. "It's a pretty majorly major deal for me. I mean, I know I'm all *famous* and everything"—Indie put a finger in her mouth and made a gagging noise—"but this is the biggest thing I've ever been cast in. I wanted to get the details right. I hadn't been a regular kid since...well, since I can't remember."

"So you went undercover at HVMS?" I said. "See how us ordinary kids walk and talk?"

"Yes, exactly," said Indie. "You don't know what it's like in Hollywood, Spartacus. I go to school sometimes but it's mostly home-tutoring. And when I *am* in school everyone else there is either in the movies or TV, or *wants* to be in movies or TV. I see more of people like Hector and Vic than anyone else, even my mom."

"You've got a mom?"

Indie rolled her Icelandic-glacier eyes and blew out a long sigh. "Oh, yeah, I've got a mom alright. If I'm ever real mad at you I'll introduce you to her. My dad's okay, but I don't see much of him. He's in movies too. A producer."

Indie sat back against the super-squishy, super-expensive leather seats. "I'm sorry I couldn't tell you about what was going on, Spartacus."

I shrugged. Tried to look like I wasn't bothered. Failed.

"If the press had got hold of it the story would've been all over the news. And my co-star in *Average Joe* is a *humongous* star. His people insisted on a total news blackout. They're going to make the announcement about the movie today. So, you see, I couldn't have told you," she said. "Plus, I wouldn't have learned a thing." She held up her black notebook.

"I always wondered what that was all about," I said. "I thought you were writing a book or something."

"I was, in a way."

Hector appeared at the window and Indie buzzed it open.

"Mr. DeMartelli said to remind you that we have an interview with Hot TV at one, Miss Starr."

Indie nodded. "One minute." She slid the window back up and turned to me.

"I've got a proposition, Spartacus."

"Oh?" I said.

"You wanna be in the movies?"

"I guess," I said.

"I want this to feel real," she said. "So that's your job. If you want it. My Production Advisor. Welcome to Hollywood, Spartacus."

CHAPTER 17

LESSON ONE

Once we got back inside Swifty's and Indie mentioned I was now on Team Starr, things got a little frosty. To say her decision wasn't welcomed by everyone would be an understatement.

No sooner had Indie gone to the bathroom when her agent, Vic "Sharknado" DeMartelli, got stuck into me. Vic was the beardy guy who, I now realized, I'd seen months back with "Kristen" in Swifty's.

He leaned over and jabbed a thick finger in my chest.

"Just so you know, kid, I'm not real keen on you hanging around. But what Indie wants, Indie gets. So you get to stay, but I'll be watchin' you. Close. Every step of the way."

Worse still was the girl in white. Phroom. Yep, that's right: just Phroom, no surname.

Phroom (I found out later) was Indie's full-time meditation and yoga assistant. She looked a lot like Indie. Like Vic, Phroom wasn't exactly what you'd call ecstatic about one R. Khatchadorian coming along for a ride on the Indie Starr Express.

"I've got my eye on you, Khatchadorian," she snarled.

I told Swifty I had had a better job offer and headed for the car. Phroom waited until Indie was safely out of earshot and cornered me next to the gum machine. "I heard all about *you*. But Indie's *mine*. Got it, buster? *Mine*. I crawled over a football field of broken glass and flames to get this job, so keep your sticky little *ordinary* paws off. *If* you want to keep 'em, that is. And remember, compared to me, Vic's a total pussycat. *Namaste*."

I realized I hadn't breathed the whole time Phroom had been speaking. I let out a long breath.

I'd just learned my first Hollywood lesson.

HOLLYWOOD 101, LESSON №1: EVERYONE IN HOLLYWOOD IS LOOKING AFTER NUMBER ONE.

CHAPTER 18

ANY CHANCE OF LUNCH WITH GEORGE CLOONEY?

Indie and her "team" headed back to Los Angeles while the movie crew started work in Hills Village. Things got hectic real quick.

Item one: Mom had asked me a bajillion questions when I got back home and, I mean, as soon as I put a toe inside the door. Someone—probably Swifty—had called her to say I'd left the diner as part of Indie Starr's entourage. She wanted to know if they'd tried any Hollywood funny business with me. I didn't know what she meant (or I pretended not to). She wanted to know if I'd signed a contract, if I was going to act in the movie, if I could get her lunch with George Clooney.

Take a wild guess at the answer.

Item two: Hills Village basically became Hollywood. If the scene at Swifty's had seemed full-on, by that evening the town was *completely* taken over by the movie people. Every hotel, motel room, spare bedroom, and cabin had been rented out. I found out later that the studio had also secretly fixed up with about twenty families to rent their houses to put up the crew. There were trailers parked across the schoolyard and guys wearing tool belts making stuff everywhere. There were helicopters. *Helicopters*. It was a total circus. It was great.

Item three: The press came to town. Loads of them. A plague. *Average Joe* was a big story, partly because Indie Starr was taking part, but mainly because of the mystery co-star. Rumors were flying around about who it could be and the press were there to see if they could find out ahead of schedule. Grandma Dotty got a scare when she found one of them rummaging around in the trash early one morning...although since Grandma Dotty was still in her nightdress (the one with the holes in it) I'm not sure who got the biggest shock.

The guy must have been trying to dig up some information on the mystery *Average Joe* star. I have no clue why he'd think there'd be anything in our trash, but I guess you'll do anything if you're desperate enough.

HOLLYWOOD 101, LESSON №2: NEVER UNDERESTIMATE HOW LOW THE PRESS WILL GO TO GET A STORY.

And *Item four*: I suddenly became popular. This is how nuts it got: Miller the Killer called up to see if I wanted to hang out. "I'll get my people to check my diary," I said.

I was *so* Hollywood already.

CHAPTER 19

CAMERA! LIGHTS! ACTION!

It was the first day of filming. I was in Indie's trailer.

I'll say that again.

I was in Indie's trailer while she was getting the final touches to her makeup. Yes, that's right: me, Rafe Khatchadorian of Hills Village, *actually inside the trailer of a real, live Hollywood star!*

And I was going over her lines with her!

And I was wearing a laminated *"Average Joe*: Access All Areas" crew pass on a lanyard! I couldn't stop stroking the shiny plastic. *Access All Areas!*

Of course, I tried to act like this was all TOTALLY NORMAL.

"What are you grinning like that for?" asked Indie. "You look like a chimpanzee with six coffees inside him. And stop stroking that crew pass, will you? You're making me nervous."

Obviously my cunning plan to act all cool and stuff was not working exactly as I'd hoped.

"Sorry," I said. I turned the script. (Yep, me, holding a real Hollywood script, in a real Hollywood trailer, with a—)

"Rafe!" snapped Indie. "You're drifting off again and you've got that big sappy grin. Concentrate!"

I concentrated. Indie had sent Vic and Phroom out of the trailer earlier so she could work on her lines with me. Vic had seemed okay with that but Phroom had looked daggers at me as she'd left.

"*Broken glass*," she'd hissed at me. "*Remember?*"

I was pretty sure me and her were not going to be buddying up anytime soon. I put thoughts of Phroom out of my head and started doing what I was supposed to be doing.

"Okay," I said, looking at the script. "So your character stands up and says...?"

The first scene was going to be one set in the classroom.

But get this: We were filming the scene in our exact classroom with most of the Hills Village kids roped in as extras. It was weird to the max. For a start, the classroom had been made more... well, *classroomy*. It looked much more like a classroom than our real classroom ever did. And everyone in the class looked like a version of themselves, only better. They were dressed better and the lighting made everyone look cool. I sort of wished HVMS looked like this all the time.

There was massive excitement on set. Today was the day we'd all find out exactly who the Big Mystery Star was. He'd been smuggled in early that morning and was in the trailer next to Indie's. His trailer was *just* that little bit bigger and *just* that little bit shinier.

There was a knock and a Megalith Movies flunky put his head round the door. "On set in five, Miss Starr," he said and disappeared.

This was it.

I collected the script with all Indie's notes in the margins. The makeup artist (everyone's an artist in the movies) swiveled Indie's chair round.

"Ready?" she said to me.

I breathed deeply. "Pretty nervous," I said.

"You'll be fine, Spartacus," said Indie. The makeup artist shook her head. Wasn't I supposed to be saying stuff like that to Indie? I made an effort to get my "cool" face on and we stepped out of the trailer.

There was a rumble of excited conversation from the extras as they caught sight of Indie. The crew didn't flicker. That, I discovered, was how it worked in the movies. Everyone thinks it's all about the actors, but the crew know it's all about them. They just carried on fixing lights, checking cameras, and generally doing all kinds of difficult-looking stuff.

I noticed Jeanne Galletta sitting in the middle of the extras. She waved to me but I didn't wave back. I was *working*. I turned to Indie and my laminated "Access All Areas" pass glinted in the lights.

I made sure Jeanne noticed it.

I SAID *ALMOND* MILK!

"**R**eady, Mr. Mordantsson?" said the floor manager.

Knut Mordantsson let out a long sigh. "Izz ze cattle ready for ze slaughterhouse? Izz ze prisoner ready for ze noose?" he said in a voice that sounded like it belonged to someone who slept in a coffin and didn't like garlic. He looked out gloomily across the classroom of extras and his shoulders sagged.

"Uh, is that a 'yes,' Mr. Mordantsson?"

Knut Mordantsson nodded slowly. "I am ready azz I will ever be. Let'z get siss nonsense over wiss."

I probably should have introduced Knut Mordantsson before but I never had a chance. Knut Mordantsson was the director of *Average Joe*.

He was a tall, really old dude (about forty), completely bald, and with a face that looked like it had been hacked out of a chunk of rock—assuming it was a really miserable-looking chunk of rock. He was from Norway, or Finland, or somewhere.

Indie told me that Knut Mordantsson would really rather be directing something depressing in black and white with subtitles, instead of this $125 million superhero movie.

I was terrified of him.

Like everyone else on the *Average Joe* set.

As Knut Mordantsson took his seat just behind the camera, there was a stirring of excitement as the door to the trailer next to Indie's opened.

"The big moment," I whispered to Indie, and she rolled her eyes.

"I can hardly wait," she said, and made a point of not looking up from her script.

A twitchy assistant stepped out of the trailer, closely followed by Indie's co-star, his face hidden in a hooded sweatshirt and baseball cap and shades. He was holding a cardboard coffee cup. The mystery star took a sip and immediately spat it out.

"I said *almond* milk, you *idiot*!" he screamed in a high-pitched voice and hurled the coffee to the floor. "What are you doing, trying to *poison* me?"

He stomped toward the set, pulled down the hood of his sweatshirt, and handed his glasses to a shaking flunky. He took off his cap and ran a hand through a head of thick, gleaming, absolutely perfect hair. "Okay, Knut baby," he said, high-fiving the director as if the coffee-throwing thing had never happened, "let's *shoot* this sucker. Right on!"

Jeanne Galletta screamed and dropped into a dead faint.

Average Joe was Trey Kernigan.

CHAPTER 21

EXPERIENCE THE WRATH OF KHATCHADORIAN KONG!

Seeing Trey Kernigan in the flesh was a bit of a shock. To say the least.

Indie caught my eye and shrugged.

"You could've told me it was *him*," I hissed in Indie's ear.

"And what good would that have done?" said Indie. "You'd just have gone all freaky about it. Kernigan's just some kid with good teeth and hair."

"I guess so," I said. "And I'm friends with *the* Indie Starr. I'm practically famous myself."

"That's right," said Indie, "you are. Now get ready because you're about to get the full Trey Kernigan experience. Here he comes."

Indie winked at me, pasted a convincing fake smile on her face, and turned round just as Trey walked across the set, bumping fists with Vic DeMartelli as he came. Well, I say "walked." It was more of a slouch and dip, slouch and dip kind of thing. He looked like he was carrying a plate of eggs in his boxers. That's the only way I can describe it.

"Why's he walking like that?" I whispered.

"Attitude," said Indie. "Trey's got *attitude*."

"*Inds!*" yelled Trey Kernigan. "Ind-*ie*, Indi-*a*, Indi-*pendent*, Indi-*vid-u-al!*"

He hugged Indie like she was his long-lost sister. I didn't get a glance.

"You put some weight on, dude?" he said, looking at Indie. "Suits you."

Indie looked at me for a fraction of a second. Her smile seemed to freeze just a little.

"Hi, Trey," said Indie. "Still doing those tooth-paste ads?"

Trey smiled, cocked his finger, and made that *click-click* sound. "Still slumming it on that small-timey Hawaii cop show?"

Before Indie could reply, the floor manager shouted, "Places, everyone, please. Going for a take."

"Good to be working with you, Inds," said Trey. "Always glad to help out a pal, give 'em a leg-up in Tinseltown." Turning away, he almost bumped into me and snapped his fingers like he'd just remembered something.

"Hey! You! Small-town hick-type dude," he said. "Go get me a soda. *Lo*-cal. And a bowl of fresh strawberries. You got strawberries out here in Hell Village, right? Make sure you wash 'em before bringing them back. I don't want any of your small-town germs. And make it snappy: some of us got work to do."

I felt my shirt rip as I instantly transformed into a gorilla. Like one of those oversize Kingy Kongy gorillas with sharp teeth and arms the size of dump trucks.

I threw my head back and pounded my gigantic chest with my equally gigantic gorilla fists. That butt-wipe Kernigan was about to experience The Wrath of Khatchadorian Kong. I was gonna tell him exactly what he could do with his *lo-cal* soda and strawberries. I was gonna rip him a new—

I froze as I caught Indie's eye.
And Vic DeMartelli's eye.
And Knut Mordantsson's eye.

And Phroom's eye, and the eyes of the cameramen and lighting crew and runners and gaffers and chippies and everyone else on set.

Basically, I caught a lot of eyes and they all seemed to be saying the same thing: *Uh-uh*. Which, if you don't know, is shorthand for "Do exactly what the Very Important Movie Star asks because all our jobs are on the line here, you idiot."

"What flavor soda?" I asked. The gorilla had gone, leaving a big fat chicken in his place. Cluck cluck cluck.

HOLLYWOOD 101, LESSON №3: THE STAR IS ALWAYS RIGHT. EVEN WHEN HE'S WRONG.

CHAPTER 22

MOVIES. TAKE. FOR. EVER

Okay, here's the thing.

By the end of that first week I'd found out a few things about the movies. Not just that the star is always right, but that movies are...kind of boring.

Whaddya mean, boring, Khatchadorian? You get to hang with stars and see the magic being made. How can that be boring?

I get it, I do. Stars, glamor, Hollywood. The whole shebang is great, but movies are *hard work*. Like real hard work. For most of the people on set. The actors do a lot of sitting around and waiting, but everyone else is on the go. All the time. Shots take FOREVER to set up and then they take it down and set up again somewhere else. Makeup has to be applied and costumes put on and continuity checked and lighting fussed around with, and then the director wants eighty-three takes of a guy saying "cheese" over and over again until he gets the exact right way of saying "cheese." Tracks laid for the cameras are always going wrong, the electricians get in the way of the carpenters, who get in the way of the teamsters, who move the heavy stuff. It's a miracle that *anything* ever comes out of all that chaos.

HOLLYWOOD 101, LESSON №4: MOVIES. TAKE. FOR. EVER.

A lot of that "magic," that Hollywood fairy dust, doesn't really happen until they get back to Los Angeles and start doing things in post.

"In post" is what we groovy movie types call everything that happens to the movie once filming has stopped: It means "post-production"... *after* production. That's when all the special effects get applied (and *Average Joe* has a ton of special effects).

So the shoot (I know all the snappy names for everything now) rolled on and on and I went home at night and came back in the morning. Indie and the rest of the Big Cheeses were all staying at different big houses the movie company had rented, but she snuck round some nights just like she used to when she was Kristen. She put on the dark wig and glasses and shook off Hector and Vic and Phroom (who was clinging to Indie like a drowning sailor to a life raft). Phroom tried every trick in the book to get between me and Indie, but Indie still managed to shake her off enough to get some time at Khatchadorian Mansions.

And it was cool when Indie came round, even if Mom did act like the Queen of England was visiting, cleaning our house until it was pretty much gleaming, like Indie hadn't been there before when the place was just a regular house. I tried telling Mom that Indie liked being in a regular house but it didn't make any difference: She just carried right on cleaning and polishing.

She also took to dropping BIG CLUNKY HINTS about me and Indie "dating." Mom made it sound like something from the olden days, and Grandma Dotty was no better.

"We're friends," I said. "Just friends. We just hang out."

"That's what they say in my magazines," said Grandma Dotty. She held up a glossy mag called

Hollywood Spice or something. "When a star starts dating someone. They always say they're 'just friends.'"

"But we *are* just friends!"

"She's got very pretty eyes," said Mom.

"Like Icelandic glaciers," I muttered and then went red.

"Busted!" said Georgia, my annoying little sister. Thanks, sis.

Of course, Indie never heard any of this stuff. As soon as she came round I made sure she interacted as little as humanly possible with my family. Total exclusion, that was the only answer. If I could've put the three of them in quarantine, I would've.

CHAPTER 23

RAFE GOES PRO

Don't tell me you bought any of that "movies are boring" stuff, did you?

Ha! Just goes to show, you can tell people anything.

I was having a ball.

For a start, I was more popular than I'd ever been in my life. And even though it was the summer vacation, I was getting the best education I'd ever had. Shelley, the *Average Joe* art director, had taken a shine to me after she saw some of my drawings. I told you there was a lot of waiting around on set. Indie didn't need me to do things all the time, so I drew stuff when I got the chance. One day Shelley asked if she could see the drawings.

"These are good, kid," said Shelley. "You ever think of doing it professionally?"

I told Shelley about my ambitions.

It felt weird thinking of it like that: "my ambitions," like I'm a grown-up already. But I *did* have ambitions. I liked art and I was pretty good at it.

"Come and see me next time you have some spare time," Shelley said. "See if we can put you to use."

The art department in a movie takes care of everything visual, or mostly everything. How a movie looks is down to the art department: what's called the "design" of the movie. The art director has a team of storyboard artists, set designers, set decorators, painters, props guys...anything that makes the movie look how it should look. On *Average Joe*, the art department had taken over the school woodwork shop as its base.

I went over there one afternoon while Knut was setting up a complicated stunt shot—which sounds more interesting than it was. Indie was in her trailer with Phroom, going through some kinda yoga-ey meditation thing, and I was definitely not invited. Not that I thought I'd be any good at yoga, or meditation. Plus Phroom had given me the Evil Eye.

Shelley looked busy but she made time for me. I was grateful. I knew from being on set just how pressured everyone was the whole time.

Shelley picked up a script. "You read this, right?"

Read it? I'd gone through it with Indie so many times I knew it off by heart. "Uh-huh," I said.

"You know that gym scene? The one where Trey gets to do a slam dunk?"

I nodded. It was my least favorite scene. Mainly because Trey comes out of it looking all heroic and stuff. I didn't mention that to Shelley.

"See if you can storyboard it for me. We had Mike do it but, I dunno, it felt a bit 'off' to me somehow. We'll use it if we don't come up with something better, but maybe you can have a go. How d'you feel about that? Okay?"

Okay? I practically danced out of the gym.

CHAPTER 24

I'LL BE IN MY TRAILER

I threw myself into the storyboard for Shelley. Every spare second I was on set when I wasn't running errands for Indie, or going over her scenes, I'd be working on the slam-dunk storyboard. I put aside my hatred for Trey "The Teeth" Kernigan and tried to come up with a scene that would make him look about as heroic as it was possible to be. It was difficult, but I was getting there. My sketchbook started filling with drawings and ideas and notes.

One strange thing about spending so much time on set and with Indie was that "real life" started seeming "unreal." Going home every night seemed like visiting a parallel universe. The thing was, it wasn't home that had changed. It was me.

One night I argued with Mom about some spaghetti being too hot or too cold or too spaghetti-like—I forget what, exactly—and I found myself storming out of the kitchen shouting, "I'll be in my trailer!"

When I was watching TV—with or without Indie—all I was doing was making comments about the shots the director had chosen.

I began getting fussy about my food. "What in the name of Charlie Christmas is silver needle

and calendula tea?" said Mom. I didn't know.
I'd only asked for it so I could be like Indie.
Phroom made that kind of stuff for her: vanilla
mushroom protein shakes, stoneground almond
butter, reishi, ho shou wu, quinton shots, mint
chip hemp milk, probiotic nori rolls with cultured
sea vegetables...I even heard them talking
about eating something called Brain Dust one
day! *Brain Dust!* I had to look it up. Turns out
it's an adaptogenic (nope, no clue) tonic made
of Astragalus (no, me neither), lion's mane (I'm
guessing that's not, like, from an actual lion),
shilajit, maca, rhodiola, and stevia.

The days passed. My drawings got better, but
in some ways I was definitely getting dumber.

HOLLYWOOD 101, LESSON №5:
BEING AROUND ACTORS TOO MUCH CAN
RESULT IN STUPIDITY.

CHAPTER 25

BULLY FOR YOU

If I'm honest, this next chapter is kind of embarrassing.

But in the interest of truth I'm gonna tell it anyway. It'll help explain what happened later.

Okay, so Indie was playing the best friend of Average Joe—which, unfortunately for Indie, meant she had to play alongside Trey in scene after scene. It had been amazing to see how smoothly Trey Kernigan could switch from full-on nastiness to all-round nice guy when the cameras started rolling. I'd seen him screaming and shouting at some assistant about *nothing* and then—*BOOM!*—ten seconds later there he was being all *likable* in a scene. I suppose that was why he earned a trillion dollars a movie. I hate to say it, but the uncomfortable fact was: Trey was a good actor.

And he knew it.

Trey never missed an opportunity to give Indie some little dig about her acting. He was like a woodpecker just tap-tap-tapping away at her confidence. I was spending hours between takes building her up only for Toothy Trey to knock her right back down again.

One time Knut had being going nuts trying to get the scene and had already reduced Indie almost to tears.

"Ve are making *Average Joe*," said Mordantsson, "not *Below Average Joe*. Now, *prepare* pleass, Miss Starr, prepare! Another take in five."

While Indie was getting herself together, out of the corner of my eye I noticed Trey shuffling the script Indie was using to check her lines. Before Indie could get herself in more trouble with Knut, I swapped the script Trey had messed with for my own copy. When Indie went straight to the right page, I could see Trey was puzzled.

There was also the time when he sent Indie off on some wild goose chase, telling her that Knut wanted to see her off the set (which, of course, he didn't). Indie was late back and Knut went knutty again.

But worst of all was the time Trey managed to stop me and Indie (cough, cough)...kissing.

HOLLYWOOD 101, LESSON №6:
BEING A BULLY IS AN ADVANTAGE IN TINSELTOWN.

CHAPTER 26

THE GREAT MOVIE STAR KISSING DISASTER

That's right, you heard me.

I almost kissed a movie star.

The key word in that sentence being *almost*.

Indie had been having another bad time of it with Trey and Knut. I can't even remember what he'd done this time (Trey, I mean) but, trust me, it was plenty lousy. It had taken me ages to talk Indie round.

"I'm thinking of quitting," she said. "This is really not working out, Spartacus."

She looked nothing like the Indie Starr her fans knew. Kind of slumped in the corner, her head resting on her hands.

"You're doing great," I said. But I didn't know what to say next. Don't blame me. I wasn't trained for this kind of thing. I didn't have a Movie Star Boosting certificate. I'd been winging it.

We were near the back of the gym, in a quiet corner where Vic or Phroom couldn't find us. They'd been trying as hard as they could to get between me and Indie, but this time we'd given them the slip. To be honest, it was more *me* giving them the slip. Indie still thought Phroom was nice. I suppose she wasn't seeing or hearing all the hissed warnings Phroom handed out in my direction. All Indie saw was the peace and love and yoga. And Vic was her agent, after all. I guess if I was in Hollywood I'd want the Sharknado in my corner.

Anyway, we were in a Vic-and-Phroom-free zone and, like I say, there was nothing I could think of to say that would make things any better, when up popped Leo.

"Kiss her, you dope," he said.

"What?"

"*Kiss* her. If you're not going to say anything, kiss her and see if that helps."

I should point out right here that if you're stuck for something to say in a conversation, the kissing option is usually NOT the one you should reach for. For a start, the person might not WANT to be kissed. You have to sort of know they want to be kissed...and, right now, that was what it felt like to me.

I decided to lean in a bit closer. If Indie leaned her face toward me that probably meant she wanted us to kiss, right? My mind calculated the exact angle of lean and distance between lips as carefully as any supercomputer.

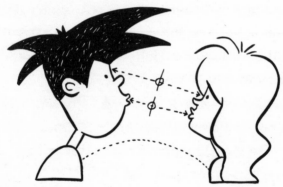

I leaned in.

And Indie leaned in.

I thought about just asking her if she thought us kissing was a good idea, but that just sounded so GIGANTICALLY lame-o that I couldn't do it. I didn't need to. Indie looked at me and I looked at Indie and our lips got closer and closer and then...I got hit smack in the side of the face by a flour bomb.

You know what a flour bomb is? Basically it's a paper bag filled with a little flour. Someone—I wonder *who* that could possibly be—had seen what was going on and decided it'd be funny to interrupt with a flour bomb.

Okay, I admit, it *could* have been quite funny if you'd been the one doing the throwing.

But I hadn't been the one doing the throwing.

I'd been the one doing the kissing, or *almost* doing the kissing. And kissing a movie star!

The flour had hit me mostly.

This is what I looked like:

Indie took one look at me and burst out laughing.

I kind of lost my temper a bit and stormed off.

I went and sat in another corner with my sketchbook and drew a big scene that involved Trey getting the sliming of his life when a GIANT vat of stinky green gloop balanced in the shadows above the basketball backboard gets triggered by Trey shooting a hoop.

It was only a revenge fantasy.

How was I to know that Knut Mordantsson would pick up my sketchbook when I went home?

CHAPTER 27

I CAN ALWAYS TELL WHEN THERE'S A "BUT" COMING

I sort of left Indie alone for a while after the whole kiss/flour thing.

I still had my laminated access pass and Indie hadn't got me thrown off the set or anything, so I hung out with Shelley as much as I could. Shelley set me up with a desk in one corner. I don't know if she'd heard about the almost-kiss, but I think she most likely had. One of the things I was learning about life on a movie set was that *everyone* knows—or wants to know—everyone else's business.

Anyway, whatever the reason, Shelley was being nice to me. She reminded me of Ms. Donatello, my art teacher. Enthusiastic.

And there was possibly another reason.

Knut was going to shoot my basketball scene.

Remember I mentioned Knut had been looking at my sketchbook? The one with my revenge slime fantasy?

Okay, well, Shelley told me that Knut had liked it.

"More than liked," said Shelley when she told me. "He went *crazy* for it, hon!"

I had a quick flash of Knut Mordantsson going crazy.

This iz not absolutely terrible...

"The gloop idea?" I said. I brightened. My idea of Trey getting super-slimed was going to happen. This was fantastic!

Shelley nodded. "We'll be working on it overnight and he's shooting it tomorrow morning. He's going to do it in top secret so he can get a real 'artistic' reaction from the actor." Shelley paused, like there was a "but" coming. I can always tell when there's a "but" coming.

"But?" I said.

"But," said Shelley, "Knut wants Indie to be the one getting slimed. And you can't tell her."

CHAPTER 28

DO YOU KNOW WHO I AM?

I didn't get much sleep that night. I couldn't stop thinking about what I was going to do about Indie and the slime scene.

I knew I *should* tell her.

Indie Starr might have been a movie star, but she was also my friend. And friends don't let friends get slimed without warning them. Was I the kind of person who'd just let that happen?

I tossed and turned. There was no way I was getting any sleep that night.

After about an hour of this, I was just about to get up and send Indie a message, warning her about the slime, when I heard a noise outside the bedroom door.

It wasn't a good noise. It sounded like something heavy and metallic being dragged across rocks. Which was kind of weird because we don't have any floors made of rock in our house. The hall outside my bedroom was just regular carpet.

"H-Hello?" I said.

My bedroom door swung open. There, silhouetted in the doorway, was a tall man dressed completely in a long black gown. A hood covered his face and in his hand he carried a scythe.

"Do you know who I am?" said the black-clad figure. His voice was deep and low, with a bit of a foreign accent. He stepped into the room and the sharp edge of his scythe glittered in the moonlight. "Most people do."

I nodded and swallowed hard. My throat felt like I'd been gargling with sand.

The black figure reached up and pulled back his hood.

"Mr. Mordantsson!" I gasped.

Knut Mordantsson looked puzzled. "Who did you ssink it vass?"

I coughed. "Er, no one," I said. "It doesn't matter." I pointed to his scythe. "What's with the scythe?"

"I like to cut grass at night. The old-fashioned way. It relaxes me when I'm filming. I always get my assistant to find me a local field. Wiss long grass."

I didn't say anything.

There isn't much you can say to something like that. But these Hollywood types do some freaky stuff. Midnight scything might be the new Big Thing in Tinseltown. What do I know?

"How did you get in?" I said.

Knut shook his head. "Ziss does not matter."

He sat down on the edge of my bed.

"What *does* matter, Mr. Khatchadorian," said Knut, "izz that Miss Starr remains unaware of what lies in store for her tomorrow." Knut ran a bony finger along the edge of the scythe. "Not. A. Vord. Izz that clear?"

I gulped and nodded.

Knut got to his feet and replaced his hood. "Exzellent," he said. He moved to the door. "I can cut my grass in peace. Goodnight, Mr. Khatchadorian."

He closed the door behind him and I listened to the scrape of his scythe handle as he dragged it across the nonexistent rock floor.

CHAPTER 29

BETWEEN A ROCK AND A HARD PLACE

I'm running.

I'm running fast and I'm in a long, dark tunnel.

And the reason I'm running fast down this long dark tunnel is that RIGHT BEHIND ME is a really big round boulder traveling at the speed of light.

Okay, that's obviously an exaggeration. But it's still going *waay* faster than I want it to. I put on a burst of speed and hurtle round a bend only to find a solid wall right in front of me.

And then I woke up sweating.

I had to tell Indie.

Except I couldn't because the Grim Reaper, aka Knut Mordantsson, told me not to. He'd even taken the trouble to stop off on the way to his midnight grass-cutting to double-check I wouldn't say a word.

Of course, all that Grim Reaper stuff hadn't happened. Not even Knut was knutty enough to do that (I think). No, I'd dreamed it all.

But (remember there's always a "but") the thing was...it *felt* real. It felt as real as Swifty's Diner, as real as Mom and Georgia and Grandma Dotty, as real as my bruises from Miller the

Killer. If I told Indie, Knut Mordantsson might just as well have actually *been* the Grim Reaper. Cross Knut and my Hollywood "career" would be dead.

I lay back on my pillow and thought about my options.

It didn't take long.

HOLLYWOOD 101, LESSON №7: LOYALTY MEANS SOMETHING DIFFERENT IN THE MOVIES.

CHAPTER 30

THE RAFE WITH NO NAME

I rested my hands on the pommel of my saddle and looked down at the dusty town from my position way up on Buffalo Ridge.

There were folks down there who needed me.

Folks who needed someone to stand up to the Grim Reaper himself.

Folks who needed a hero.

I spat out a wad of chewing licorice, pulled down the brim of my battered cowboy hat, and squinted my eyes against the desert sun. I checked I had my trusty six-shooter on my hip and a full canteen of vinegar and orneriness. I looked at my knuckles. They carried the scars of a dozen bar-room brawls (and that was only last week). If things got bad in town I might have to show the Grim Reaper my Two-Fist Special.

"C'mon, Lightnin'," I growled, and leaned back as Lightning slowly picked his way toward Hills Village and my date with destiny.

I was going to tell Indie and nothing was going to stop me.

RAFE KHATCHADORIAN: DRAGON SLAYER, SMOOTHIE RUNNER

The first person I saw when I got to the set was Phroom. She was standing just inside one of the security gates that kept the ordinary people off the set. Since I had my "Access All Areas" pass, I breezed through without a problem.

Phroom being there was kind of odd because, as you might have noticed, Phroom never strayed more than ten feet from Indie if she could help it.

"Hi, Rafe," said Phroom, smiling pleasantly. "What's up?"

Phroom's smile could only mean one of two things. One: She'd turned over a new leaf and wanted to be best buds with me. Or two (far more likely): Phroom knew what I was going to do and wanted to head me off at the pass. I knew enough about how things worked around there that Phroom might have got wind of Knut's secret slime scene... and had somehow guessed I'd want to warn Indie.

It wasn't too hard to see how her mind was working: Let Indie get slimed, Indie blames Rafe for not warning her, Phroom is back in as Indie's Number Two. Simple.

"You're not going to stop me that easy," I said. "I'm going to tell Indie."

Phroom's smile vanished. "I have no idea what you're talking about," she hissed, and stomped off in the direction of the trailers.

I smiled grimly. I felt like I'd slain my first dragon.

I replaced my sword in its scabbard and marched on toward Indie.

The next obstacle in my path was a shark. Vic DeMartelli. When I came round the corner he'd been talking to Phroom, his arms moving round like a wind-up toy. As soon as they saw me they broke apart and Vic headed in my direction.

From the look on Vic's face, he was not going to be as easy to get past as Phroom had been. For a start, he had hold of my arm in a grip like iron.

"You got a minute, kid?" said Vic. "I need you to run an errand."

I held up a hand. "No problem, Mr. DeMartelli," I said. "But first I have to tell Indie something before they shoot the next scene."

Vic sucked his lower lip like he was eating a lemon. For a second I thought he was going to have me rubbed out. Then he seemed to recover and replaced his lip-sucking lemon face with something he must have thought looked friendly. He looked about as friendly as a gorilla with toothache.

"Tell her what?" said Vic.

Ah. Okay, here's the thing: It's okay for me to tell Indie that she's about to get slimed, because I'm her friend, but it's not okay for me to tell Vic that, because Knut swore me to secrecy.

I think. Either way, it didn't feel right telling Vic. Plus, a little bit of me wanted to be the one to warn Indie. Be the hero or something, I don't know.

"It's Indie who wants you to get her something," said Vic. "She needs you to bring her a flugella and caspardiem smoothie."

"A what?"

"A flugella and caspardiem smoothie. It's a thing. Ask the guy in catering. You got plenty of time to speak to Indie before filming starts, so don't get your undies in a twist. Okay, scram, vamoose, go."

I looked over in the direction of the gym. Things were happening over there. I heard the floor manager start saying the kind of things he'd say just before a scene started shooting. I didn't have much time to get this smoothie. Plus, I wasn't sure if Vic was sending me on this errand to get me out of the way. He'd just been talking to Phroom and the whole thing looked pretty suspicious from my angle. But what could I do except go? If I refused, Vic would want to know why and I couldn't tell him without spilling the beans. The only thing I could do was go get this smoothie and get back before the scene started. It wasn't a great plan, but it was the best I could come up with at short notice.

"Tell Indie not to go on set before she's spoken to me," I said, and then ran for the catering truck like my life depended on it.

Which it did.

WE ARE AT DEFCON 5

"**A** *what?*"

The guy behind the counter at the catering truck looked at me like I was nuts.

"A flugella and caspardiem smoothie. It's for Miss Starr?"

"I don't care if it's for the President," said the catering guy. "It don't exist, son. Someone's been playing a joke on you."

I turned and ran.

This was no joke.

"Quiet on set!"

I skidded to a halt as I came round the corner into the gym. The soles of my sneakers squeaked on the polished floor and a bunch of people looked at me and frowned.

"Complete quiet!"

Knut Mordantsson shifted in his chair and gave me a Scandinavian Death Stare. It was a bit like Phroom's but with added Viking. He looked scarier than he had in my Grim Reaper nightmare. I spotted Vic and Phroom watching from the shadows. The basketball court—the part of it being used in the scene—was brightly lit and there in the center were Indie and Trey, both in costume. I looked up above the basketball backboard and could just make out the hidden gloop vat. Two members of the crew were in place on either side of it, ready to tip. It was all exactly as I'd sketched out.

Indie sort of half noticed me, I think.

I signaled with my eyes that she was about to get slimed, but that's a pretty hard thing to do in a brightly lit room standing two feet from another person. Across a darkened movie set it was impossible.

"And let's go for a take," said the floor manager. He looked at Knut, who nodded.

"Unt *action*," said Knut.

I was too late.

THE CREATURE FROM
GREEN GLOOP SWAMP

I have to admit, Knut had a point about keeping the glooping secret from Indie.

If all you cared about was the movie. Which I didn't...at least not as much as the rest of them did.

Here's how it all went down...

The first take didn't get to the glooping stage. In the script Indie's supposed to grab the basketball, take a shot, miss, and then Trey takes over and does a little "demonstration" of his amazing b-ball skills. Hurp.

On the first take Indie fluffed a line. I hoped there might be some sort of waiting around for the next take and I'd get a chance to warn her, but it didn't happen. They reset and went for take two. I still had a chance. As long as Indie didn't make the hoop there'd be no gloop.

Trey and Indie swapped lines and then Indie grabbed the basketball. She gave Trey the line and set herself up for the shot.

I don't know if Indie was aiming to miss or aiming to score but the ball sailed sweetly through the air and dropped with a soft swish through the hoop.

Indie turned and, before she could say a word, was hit from above by three hundred gallons of lime green gloop. There was so much of the stuff

that she was knocked off her feet and was carried across to the edge of the court like a surfer on a wave.

It was incredible.

It was astonishing.

It was The Greatest On-Screen Glooping Ever Seen.

Knut was happy. "Yess," he said. "Cut zere. Izz satissfactory."

Indie was in deep shock. This is what she looked like:

I looked at Indie. Indie looked at me. Then Indie looked toward Phroom, who was holding up my sketchbook. The one with the whole glooping scene sketched out in every last detail...

Indie looked back at me. "How *could* you?" she gasped.

My movie days were over.

CHAPTER 34

BANiSHMeNT

The Elf Lord Mordantsson rolled out the length of parchment. Standing on the battlements of Castle Holy Wood at the very edge of the Kardashian Kingdom, and speaking in a clear voice that carried across the heads of the assembled Nurfgurts, he read out the punishment:

"For disloyalty to Her Most Royal Highness Indiana Starr, disgraced hobbit scribe Rafe Khatchadorian izz hereby banished forthwith and forever from Filmanteevee Land..."

A single drumbeat boomed out and the Holy Wood gates creaked open. Rafe Khatchadorian swallowed hard. There was nothing out there except an endless dust-blown desert populated by Killer Millers and Dragon Principals.

"Please," Rafe begged as the Hectorian Guards dragged him away. "Please let me stay! I don't want to leave! I'll be *good*, I swear! Just let me stay in Filmanteevee Land..."

As you'll have figured from all that, Indie didn't calm down after her glooping.

In fact, she got madder, and it was Indie who demanded Knut throw me off the set. Knut and Vic cornered me about eighteen seconds after Phroom led Indie back to her trailer. Hector the bodyguard stood behind them.

"You gotta go, kid," said Vic. He shrugged. "When the talent doesn't want you around, well, that's it."

"But it was you who sent me for that flugella smoothie!" I said.

"What izz *flugella*?" said Knut. "I never have heard off ziss."

"Exactly," I said. "Vic sent me away so I wouldn't tell Indie she was going to get slimed!"

"I thought I'd asked you *not* to tell Miss Starr about the slime?" said Knut. "Ziss wass an extremely expensive shot we make in ziss moment, yes? I needed Miss Starr to react as she did, so it izz a *good* thing you didn't tell her. Vic did you and me a favor, Mr. Khatchadorian."

Knut patted Vic on the back and Vic nodded shyly, like he was some kind of war hero or something.

"Someone's got to pay," said Knut, "unt I am afraid it izz you."

"It's not fair!" I said.

"Welcome to Hollywood," said Vic.

HOLLYWOOD 101, LESSON №8:
IN THE MOVIES, "FAIR" IS A HAIR COLOR.

CHAPTER 35

WATCH OUT FOR THE FLYING ZOMBIE-MONKEYS

I spent most of the next week in my cave being miserable. I was good at it, and the longer I was in my room, the better at it I got.

Mom, Grandma Dotty, Georgia, and Leo all made big efforts to get me to come out, but I was going to stay in my cave forever and that's all there was to it. My getting booted off the set was all over Hills Village. (I still had my computer so I wasn't entirely cut off from the outside world.) *What a loser* was about the nicest thing anyone was saying about me. Maybe I shouldn't have been quite so proud of my "Access All Areas" laminate? Rumors were flying around about why I'd been booted off, but no one knew the real reason. Megalith Movies was keeping the *Average Joe* super-slime sequence under wraps until the movie was out. I had thought about spilling the beans to the press, but Knut had warned me not to. He said if I mentioned a single word about Indie being slimed he'd send a plague of carnivorous flying zombie-monkeys after me. Or possibly lawyers.

He might have said lawyers.

Life *sucked*.

I was one of the ordinary people again.

THAT'S A WRAP

In the end, I did come out of the cave.

There's only so long you can shut yourself away, because it gets kind of boring, no matter how miserable you want to be. Besides, I was missing what was left of the summer, even if that did mean facing going back to working in Swifty's and dealing with the people in HV who didn't like me.

Which was pretty much everyone.

The *Average Joe* crew had gone. "My" slime scene had been one of the last ones they shot, and the entire production had slipped out of town without leaving a trace. I was beginning to think the whole thing had been a dream. Or possibly a nightmare—I couldn't decide. One minute I was besties with a movie star, the next I'm back swabbing grease off the dishes in Swifty's. Some summer.

I'd been following the progress of *Average Joe* online and it looked like it was going to make a trillion dollars or something. Indie's glooping had been leaked online and went viral. It'd become a thing; up there with videos of farting cats and surfing chickens. A "glooping" trend had started with people glooping other people all over the place.

And there were rumors that Indie Starr and Trey Kernigan were now "an item." Like I said, some summer.

"Hey, Hollywood!" yelled Swifty. "Get your head back on the job!"

"Hollywood" was now my nickname at the diner.

I plunged my hands back into the deep, black, scummy water and thought deep, black, scummy thoughts.

CHAPTER 37

APOLOGY NUMBER ONE

Here's another of those time-travel *FRRRRP*s coming up. Ready? Okay.

FRRRRRRRRRRP!

One Tuesday night, three months later...

I was back at school. I don't need to tell you all the other stuff about how I felt and all that kind of thing because once I said the words "I was back at school" you'd know *exactly* how I was feeling.

Anyway, like I said, it was a Tuesday night. I was kind of half watching a rerun of an old TV show: *Hawaii Surf Squad*. Yep, the one with Miss Indie Starr playing the daughter of one of the Hawaii PD detectives. Don't judge me.

Indie had just helped solve who had killed one

of the judges in the big surf competition when the phone rang. My phone, I mean, not Indie's in *Hawaii Surf Squad*.

"Is that Rafe?" said a voice.

It was Shelley, the *Average Joe* art director.

I played it cool. "Hey," I said. Iceman or what? It was Shelley, after all, who had said zip when I got the boot off *Average Joe*. Shelley knew I'd been put in an impossible position: either ratting out by telling Indie she was going to get glooped, or saying nothing and betraying a friend. I wasn't going to let her get off easy without, I don't know, apologizing or something.

"I called to apologize," said Shelley. "I should have said something when Mordantsson kicked you off the movie. I'm sorry."

Oh, okay. I immediately had to reorganize all my sarcastic responses.

"Well, a lot of people could have said something," I said. "And Knut was your boss. You'd have been fired."

"Maybe. Or maybe I might have just stood up to him for once. It's not something I'm proud of, Rafe. But the movie business is a bit like that."

I nodded. Which was kind of dumb because I was on the phone. "Sure," I said.

"Listen," said Shelley. "How'd you like to come and do some work at the studio? Our place, I mean: MesaMovieArts."

"Like an intern?"

"Exactly," said Shelley. "Next vacation period we'll fix it up. I'll talk to your mom. You can stay with me and my family. Flights on me, okay?"

I didn't know what to say.

"This is where you say, 'Thank you, Shelley,'" said Shelley.

"Thank you, Shelley," I said.

"Okay, kid, that's great! Looking forward to it! Oh, and listen, you don't need to beat yourself up about Indie. Turned out the whole thing was a fake."

"A fake?"

"Yep. Vic had told Indie about the glooping. Vic, Trey, and Indie all thought it'd look great on YouTube. Thought it'd really help boost the movie, and they were right. So, you see, Indie knew all about it. So long, Rafe. Speak soon. Ciao."

Say *what*?

I looked at the phone like I was expecting it to give me more information. It didn't. Obvs.

Indie was in on the glooping all along?

This was going to take some serious thinking about.

HOLLYWOOD 101, LESSON №9: THERE IS NO SUCH THING AS BAD PUBLICITY.

CHAPTER 38

THE ICEMAN COMETH

S helley's call wasn't the only excitement I got that week. Two days later, I was finishing up my morning at Swifty's when I saw a familiar face in one of the booths.

Indie.

Except this wasn't Indie. It was Kristen: dark wig, glasses, bangs.

But Indie or Kristen, I wasn't ready to talk to either of them just yet.

I have to admit, when I saw Indie—I'm gonna stick with "Indie" even if she was dressed like "Kristen"—my stomach flipped. I mean, I didn't puke or faint or anything, but it was a weird feeling all the same. My legs felt like jello, but I took a deep breath. I was going to be the Iceman if it killed me.

"What are you going to do?" asked Leo.

"I'm not going to do anything," I said, "except ignore her."

"Just sail right past her like she's not there?" Leo nodded approvingly. "The old breezeroo. Nothing like it."

"She's going to get ignored like she's never been ignored before," I said. "The Iceman is gonna show Indie Starr exactly what 'cool' means." I lifted my chin high, set my face to "Arctic," and headed for the door, my eyes fixed dead ahead. No looking right, no looking left. Hollywood star or no Hollywood star, I wasn't going to—

BOOOOMFF! I walked right into a bucket Swifty had been using to mop up a spill from a table.

It was spectacular. My right foot went straight into the bucket, sending me sliding across the floor and into a table piled high with breakfast specials. I planted my face smack into a stack of pancakes, and knocked about eighteen gallons of

coffee all over three members of the Hills Village
Benevolent and Protective Order of Elks. Their
screams could be heard on Pluto.

As Swifty hauled me out of old Murchison's
lap, managing somehow to call me every
name under the sun *and* apologize to the Elks
individually *while* mopping up the worst of the
damage, I risked a glimpse at Indie's booth.

She'd gone.

CHAPTER 39

APOLOGY NUMBER TWO

The only good thing about my whole foot-in-bucket disaster was that Indie hadn't seen it. I guessed she must have gone to the bathroom during the action and missed the whole thing. Or maybe she'd been teleported up to an alien spaceship, or hadn't been in Swifty's at all. Maybe I was seeing things. Whatever it was, I was glad my shame hadn't been witnessed.

"You been practicing that?" said a voice as I trudged out of Swifty's. "Because I have to say, you got it just perfect, Spartacus."

I looked up.

Indie Starr was leaning against the wall by the steps into Swifty's.

"Very funny," I said and started walking.

"Wait," said Indie.

I ignored her. I still owed her some ignoring. I'd much rather she'd got the ignoring back in Swifty's but I was too mad to care now.

Indie put her hand on my shoulder.

"Please, Spartacus," she said.

I stopped.

"I'm sorry," said Indie. She leaned forward and plucked a piece of scrambled egg off my ear. "Really, I am. Even though it was all your idea, I should have told you I knew about the glooping."

"It wasn't my idea to gloop you! I tried to tell you!"

"I know," said Indie. "So I've come with a peace offering." She pointed toward a black limo tucked around at the side of Swifty's. Hector was in the driving seat and he gave me a small salute.

"Come to the *Average Joe* premiere with me," she said. "It's in a couple of days' time. Vic's squared everything with your mom. She gave us a suitcase with your clothes and stuff and we'll fix up everything else. There's a private jet waiting to fly us to LA. All you got to do is say 'yes' and get in the car."

I thought about it.

Indie and Phroom and Trey and Vic and Knut had all been double-lousy to me in one way or another. I'd been lied to, threatened, used, and then tossed away like a half-eaten flugella and caspardiem sandwich. I was the laughing stock of Hills Village Middle School and my confidence was shattered. Was I just going to let some movie star buy me off by waving a shiny ticket to a Hollywood premiere in front of me?

"Yeah!" I said. "I'm in!"

Indie smiled and kissed me.

"But give me an hour," I said. "I have to make a couple of calls."

CHAPTER 40

HOLLYWOOD TAKEDOWN

It was the world premiere of *Average Joe*.

Our limo slid to a halt outside Grauman's Chinese Theatre in Los Angeles. Through the window I could see the full Hollywood thing going on: red carpet, paparazzi, flashing cameras, screaming fans, the works.

The door opened and I stepped out. I was wearing a suit and tie that Indie had got me from a fancy clothes shop. Even though the collar felt too tight, I looked good.

"For once," said Leo.

"Look who's talking, parka boy," I whispered. "Now scram." The last thing I needed tonight was some paparazzi getting a shot of me talking to my imaginary brother.

Behind me, Indie stepped out of the limo with Trey Kernigan.

Yeah, I didn't mention that. Bit of a downer, but Indie had explained it was all part of the game.

"It's in the contract," she'd said. "We arrive at the premiere together. Buddy up for the cameras. Smile, act like we're all one big, happy family."

And that's what was happening. Trey was beaming his big zillion-watt smile and lapping up all the screaming like it was exactly what he deserved.

Indie looked great, by the way. I should mention that too. She was wearing a long, shiny black dress that probably cost as much as a small country. She was also giving everyone the full Indie Starr smile. Next to her and Trey, I looked like some dude who'd wandered in off the street.

Which wasn't far off how I felt. Everywhere I looked famous people were talking and laughing with other famous people. I saw...well, let's just say I saw *everyone*.

"Pretty wild, huh, kid?" said Vic DeMartelli. "Just keep grinning and you'll keep winning!"

Vic moved past me and shook hands with eight people at once. I don't know how he did that. Vic was working the red carpet. That's what they call it: *working*. It means waving and smiling and talking to the press people as you inch toward the doors. Since no one was remotely interested in me, this part of it was pretty easy.

Phroom was there too, natch, standing off to one side like a well-dressed spider.

As soon as I came in range she fired off an Extra-Evil Phroom Death Stare but, thanks to my newly installed Complete Hollywood Insanity Force-Field, it bounced off harmlessly. "*Namaste*, Phroom," I said, bowing, and getting a full-strength scowl in return.

I was getting the hang of Hollywood.

"Mr. Khatchadorian." Looking like he was at a funeral, Knut Mordantsson loomed up into view and shook my hand. "Vot a circus," he said, waving a hand at the photographers and screaming fans. "It dissgusstss me."

Knut moved on toward the big arch that stretched over the entrance to the theater. There was a kind of mini-stage set up there for the official photographer to get photos of all the celebs. The cast of *Average Joe*, plus Knut and Phroom (who elbowed her way in as close as she could get to Indie), were herded together like shiny sheep.

About twenty yards back I stopped to tie my shoelace. Glancing up to the top of the arch, I glimpsed someone moving. It was Tommy, one of Shelley's crew, standing next to a huge vat. He caught my eye and raised a hand in question.

"Do it," said Leo. I stood and gave Tommy a thumbs-up.

WOW!

TRIPLE WOW!

Tommy flipped a switch, and more green gloop than had ever been put in one place tipped straight onto the *Average Joe* cast.

It. Was. *SPECTACULAR!*

Indie got glooped. Trey Kernigan got glooped. Knut Mordantsson got glooped. Phroom got glooped and washed all the way back to Hollywood Boulevard on a tidal wave of gloop. The red carpet got glooped, the spectators got glooped, the press got glooped, the limos got glooped, and even I got glooped. *Average Joe* had been well and truly glooped.

And none of them suspected a thing.

HOLLYWOOD 101, LESSON №10: TRUST NO ONE: ESPECIALLY YOUR FRIENDS....

EPILOGUE

"Worked like a dream," I said, looking at the news coverage of the *Average Joe* Great Green Gloop premiere disaster. The clip of the impact was played over and over again.

The glooping story was the lead on every channel and was the highest-trending thing on the planet. The video had already been watched about eighty-six million times.

"You said it," said Vic DeMartelli, leaning back in his office chair, his hands behind his head and smiling the smile of a Hollywood agent with a humongous hit on his hands. "Great idea! Indie and Trey never suspected a thing!" Vic looked at me proudly, the way a father looks at his newborn son, and a single tear trickled down his cheek. "So sneaky! So, so, *so* sneaky!" he said, brushing the tear from his face, his voice choked with emotion. "You've got a great future in this town, kid!"

HOLLYWOOD 101, LESSON №11:
AFTER A NUCLEAR WAR, ONLY THREE CREATURES WILL SURVIVE—COCKROACHES, BACTERIA, AND HOLLYWOOD AGENTS.

IF IT WEREN'T FOR ROTTEN LUCK, RAFE KHATCHADORIAN WOULDN'T HAVE ANY LUCK AT ALL!

READ ON FOR A SNEAK PEEK

THIS IS NOT A DRILL

E ver since I've known you—how long has it been now?—I've been getting my butt kicked in about a hundred different ways. Well, the butt-kicking officially stops here.

On this page.

Before the next period

•

That's why this could be my best story yet. I've got a ton of stuff to tell you about. More than ever, in fact. For a while, I thought maybe I'd call this book *The Butt-Kick Stops Here*. Or maybe *Look at Me, I'm Special*. Or *First Kiss*. Or *Rafe Khatchadorian: Secret Agent Artist*.

But I didn't call it any of those things. In case you haven't already noticed, I called this one *Just My Rotten Luck*.

And even though that doesn't sound like the happy-go-luckiest title you've ever heard of (with plenty of good reason), there's a lot that happens in this book that's pretty awesome.

Like me being a football hero.

Yeah, yeah. I know *football* and *Rafe Khatchadorian* don't exactly go together like ham and eggs. But that really was me, hitting the field for the Hills Village Middle School Falcons. It really did happen.

Really, really.

Don't get me wrong. I'm not saying this story is going to be all about touchdowns and cheerleaders screaming my name. (*Obviously*. I mean, have you seen what I look like?)

I'm just saying…well, you know what? Maybe I should start at the beginning. And for that to happen, we have to go back in time a little bit. And *that* means I'm going to need a good old-fashioned flashback. Then a flash-forward, and then who knows what else after that.

So buckle up, people. It's going to be a bumpy ride. All set? Good.

Here comes the flashback!

CHAPTER 2

ROUGH START

Welcome to THE PAST! Don't worry, we didn't go that far. Just three weeks earlier, to be exact.

I was at the tail end of a pretty lousy summer, which is *supposed* to be the best time of the year for most kids. Me, not so much. Camp Wannamorra had been a disaster, and my time at The Program in the Rocky Mountains just about killed me in six different ways. (Well, okay, just *one* way, but still…)

None of that was the worst part, though. That happened on the Friday before school started, when Mom took me to Hills Village Middle School. We had a meeting scheduled with Mrs. Stricker and Mrs. Stonecase so I could get re-enrolled there.

You remember Mrs. Stricker, right? And Mrs. Stonecase too? They're the principal and vice principal of HVMS. They're also sisters—for real. That's like getting twice the trouble for half the price. Not to mention, if there was a Worldwide Khatchadorian Haters Club, they'd be the president and vice president.

So anyway, as soon as I was stuck inside that lion's den (I mean, sitting down in Mrs. Stricker's office), I got a two-ton piece of bad news dropped on my head.

"If Rafe wishes to come back to Hills Village Middle School this fall," Mrs. Stricker said to my mom, "he'll have to be enrolled as a special needs student."

And I was like, "Say WHAT?"

But Stricker wasn't done. She kept going, like a tidal wave of meanness that just couldn't be stopped. "Whether he'll finish middle school on time or have to put in an extra semester or two—or *more*—well, we just can't say at this point," she told us.

And then I was like, "Say WHAAAAAAT???"

I don't know what they call it at your school. IEP. SPED. Special Education. Barnum & Bailey's Three-Ring Circus. At HVMS, the kids have plenty of names for it—just not ones they say when any teachers are around.

And now I was in it.

I tried to talk Stricker, Stonecase, and even Mom out of making this horrible mistake, but they wouldn't budge. Mom wasn't being mean about it or anything. I know she wants what's best for me. She just said I should give it a try.

"We'll see how things go once the school year starts," she said. "Who knows, maybe you'll even like it."

Which is such a MOM thing to say.

In the meantime, if you're thinking this story is all about bad news, don't worry. Some cool stuff happens too, like that first kiss, and some other things I haven't even told you about yet.

But so far? My school year was off to the worst start ever.

And it hadn't even started yet.

Other books in the Middle School series

Hey guys!
Don't miss my
next hilarious
adventure,
Dog's Best Friend!

Available 20th October 2016